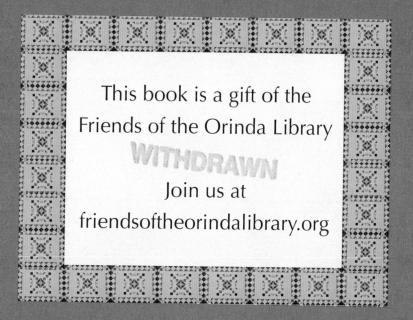

Another one for my friend Jean-Guillaume...
Why change a winning team!

Published in North America in 2014 by Owlkids Books Inc.

Published in France under the title *La course* in 2012 by Éditions Milan.

Owlkids Books acknowledges the financial support of the Canada Council for the Arts, the Ontario Arts Council, the Government of Canada through the Canada Book Fund (CBF) and the Government of Ontario through the Ontario Media Development Corporation's Book Initiative for our publishing activities.

Published in Canada by	Published in the United States by
Owlkids Books Inc.	Owlkids Books Inc.
10 Lower Spadina Avenue	1700 Fourth Street
Toronto, ON M5V 2Z2	Berkeley, CA 94710

Library and Archives Canada Cataloguing in Publication

Manceau, Édouard, 1969- [Course. English]   The race / Édouard Manceau.

Translation of: La course. Translation by Sarah Quinn. ISBN 978-1-77147-055-1 (bound)

   I. Quinn, Sarah, translator II. Title. III. Title: Course. English.

PZ7.M333Ra 2014   j843'.92   C2013-905488-X

Library of Congress Control Number: 2013949120

Manufactured in Shenzhen, Guangdong, China, in October 2013, by WKT Co. Ltd.
Job #13CB1605

A   B   C   D   E   F

Owl kids   Publisher of Chirp, chickaDEE and OWL
www.owlkidsbooks.com

THE RACE

Édouard Manceau

Owl
kids

It begins with a guy, a can
of paint, and a paintbrush.

Then he grabs a megaphone
and gives a loud shout.

That brings a bunch of other guys
who start bending and twisting.

Then the first guy comes back with
a pistol, and everyone freezes.

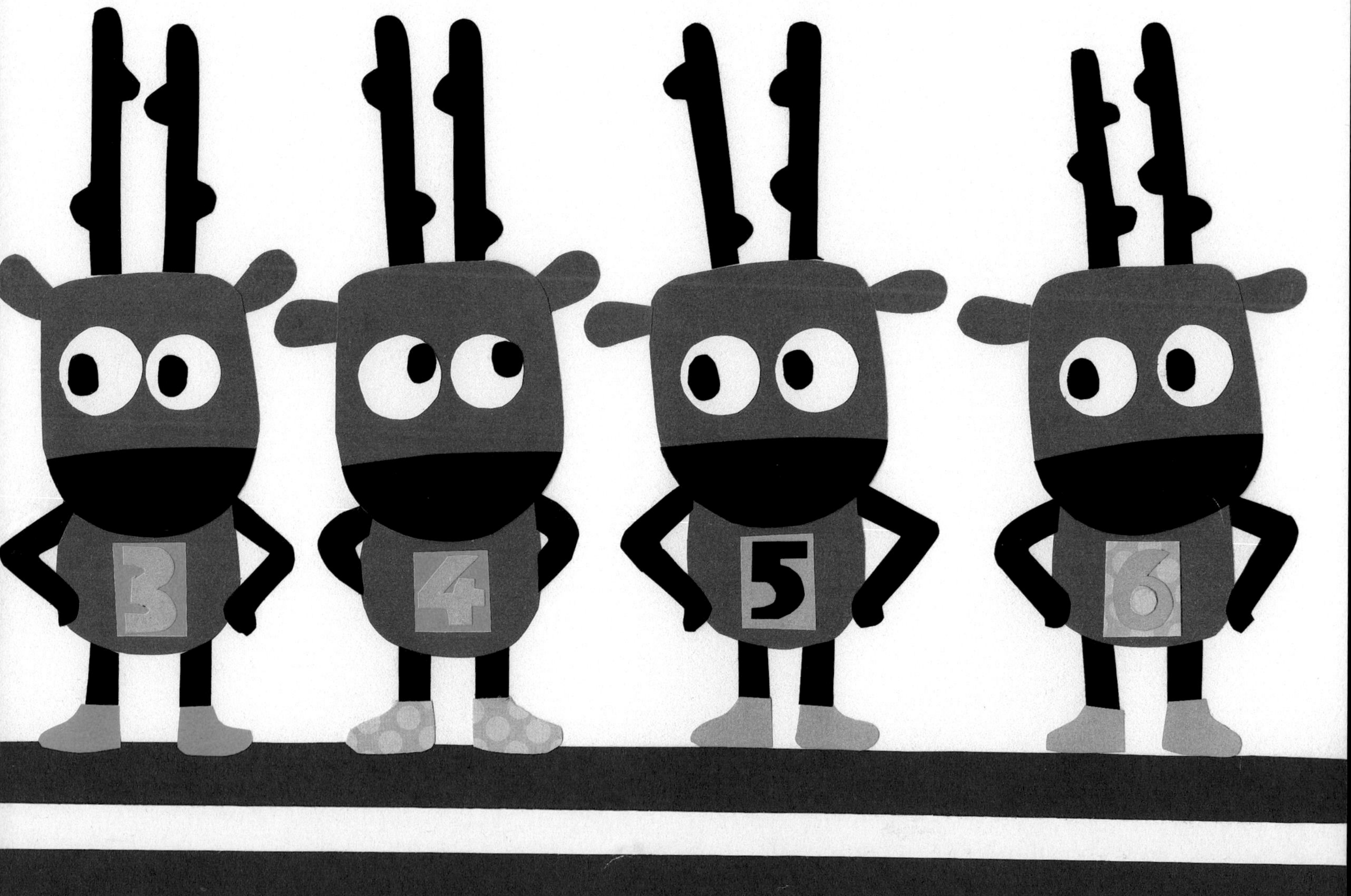
3
4
5
6

Sometimes, one of them
tries to get away.

It doesn't usually take long to catch him.
That's called a false start.

Then everyone lines up again,
nice and straight.
The first guy fires the pistol,
and everyone else runs away.

There's always one guy who takes off full tilt, without waiting for the others. He must really want to be first.

And to stay first, he'll try anything—
even the infamous banana-peel trick.

Which works every time.

That's when they call in
the medics to fix everyone up.

Quitting is not an option!
Once they're patched up, the banana-peel
survivors hit the ground running.

They'll do anything to catch up
to the banana-peel guy.

Really, anything...

And that's how
Mr. Banana Peel
learns to fly.

In the meantime,
the rest of the guys refuel.

And then they're off again!

It gets harder and harder.

Some guys can't take it
and would rather stop.

They wonder why they started
running like that in the first place.

So they decide to
settle down, enjoy life.

The others don't give it much thought.
They keep playing tricks on each other...

Even really nasty ones!

In the end, one guy throws his arms high in the air, because he's the first to cross a nice new line.

They give him flowers, they clap,
they put him on TV, and they
call him the champion.
Everyone says that he has won.

They say there is only one winner.
They also say that everyone else lost.
But that...

...that's just what they say.